THE LAST PASSPORT TO HEAVEN

THE LAST PASSPORT TO HEAVEN

▼

The Tale of an Adventurous Spirit Who Traveled to Heaven and Back

Larry Richardson

with illustrations by Gregory Richardson

Writers Club Press

San Jose New York Lincoln Shanghai

The Last Passport to Heaven
The Tale of an Adventurous Spirit Who Traveled to Heaven and Back

Writers Club Press
an imprint of iUniverse.com, Inc.

For information address:
iUniverse.com, Inc.
5220 S 16th, Ste. 200
Lincoln, NE 68512
www.iuniverse.com

This is in most part a work of fiction. Although inspired by an actual event the names, persons and characters are inventions of the author. Any resemblance to people living or deceased is purely coincidental. This book includes a compliation of quotations collected over the years by the author. Reasonable effort has been made to identify the original author of the quoted material. The author welcomes readers to autheticate an oversight for a future correction.

ISBN: 0-595-18823-0

Printed in the United States of America

DEDICATION

Gale & Dora Richardson

They both had their Passports to Heaven and I know they took extra ones to share along the way. My parents first showed me this amazing creation 35 years ago and so I honor them by carrying their message with me into the future.

Dora   1920–1993
Gale   1919–1998

EPIGRAPH

"Children are the living messages we send to a time we will not see."

—Neil Postman—

CONTENTS

PREFACE

A HELPFUL MESSAGE
To All Potential Readers of This Book

To fully enjoy the message of this book and to experience just how amazing the "Last Passport to Heaven" is, I ask you, to please begin reading from front to back. If you peek ahead in this book you will probably diminish the magic for yourself.

Can you resist the temptation?
Please try not to peek ahead in this book

I have provided instructions in a specific order for your experience to be fully realized. If you faithfully follow these instructions you will be well rewarded as the secret of "The Last Passport to Heaven" unfolds for you. This is one of those things that must be seen to be believed.

More than a book, this is an experience

in which you actively participate.

You will learn by doing.

You'll never look at a blank piece of paper the same way again. How can something so simple create something so special, and so memorable?

Before continuing locate a blank sheet of 8½ by 11 inch white paper — it is critical to this story.

ACKNOWLEDGEMENTS

I am grateful to my family and to the many friends whose encouragement, and assistance made this book possible.

Gregory Richardson M.D. for valuable assistance in crystallizing the concepts and ideas presented in this book along with the great diagrams he created to assist the reader.

To my niece Dawn Richardson who was inspired to reveal another revelation in the "The Last Passport to Heaven," on Thanksgiving Day 1996. She proved that the "Passport" is a work in progress.

To Susan Stuart who first read this manuscript and offered her editing and concept assistance.

To those who have left us the wisdom I used to add inspiration to this tale of adventure, faith and the willingness to share.

Finally to my daughter Brie who at the age of three asked me her first profound questions. Dad, where does God come from? I replied, "That is one of the great riddles in life. Solve that riddle and you will be more famous than your Barbie." My daughter then asked me "Dad, where does Barbie come from?"

INTRODUCTION

What would you do if you suddenly died and found yourself standing outside the gates of Heaven? Would you be prepared? Would you have the wisdom to do what is right if you were tested time and time again?

What if the guardian of the gate, Saint Peter, came up to you with his hand outstretched and asked you this one question?

"May I see your Passport to Heaven please?"

Would you start laughing out loud? Would you be speechless? Would you be wondering what on Earth you were doing without a celestial passport at a time like this?

Well, for both Heaven's sake and your own, please don't stop reading this book. All these questions and many more will be answered by the time you finish this manuscript.

This book resulted from a personal journal kept by my close friend Aaron. I have faithfully brought his journal to life and hope that you are as amazed as I was with what you are about to read. **Remember:** before continuing on with this story, please have a blank sheet of 8½ by 11 inch white paper available.

A Message From Aaron

My name is Aaron. I am about to share with you the story of an incredible journey I took from one paradise, my home in Hawaii, to another paradise, that almost defies description, a paradise known to millions of us as Heaven.

I have been given the inspiration to have this book published, and to share with you the knowledge I received of "The Last Passport to Heaven." What I am about to show you excites me and what will happen when you share what you learn with others is amazing.

I have tried to share the best highlights of my journey, and I will admit that at times the story moves quickly. I was so eager to record what I had learned that I wrote furiously in my journal until I was exhausted.

If I have been able to sow a few seeds of expectation in you, then you are ready to follow me on the journey of a lifetime.

What follows is a faithful transcription directly from Aaron's journal. Aaron's experience was recorded on a quiet starlit night in July, in Hawaii, on the Island of Oahu, in his home located on the slopes of the peaceful, green, Manoa Valley.

CHAPTER 1

▼

AARON'S STORY...THE BEGINNING

"I'm not afraid of dying. I just don't want
to be there when it happens"

—*Woody Allen*—

When I look back upon what occurred earlier this evening, I wonder what in the world happened to me. Did I die? Was it a vision? Or was it the most thought-provoking dream of my life?

I do know for sure that what I saw and experienced woke up my soul. I am compelled to record these experiences, and to share them with you before my memory of them is lost.

As I was preparing for bed earlier this evening I opened a drawer in my nightstand and removed my personal journal, which contained a listing of "My Words for Life." It was a statement by Winston Churchill that inspired me to create a collection of single words that would energize me with their positive power. Churchill believed that what really mattered in his life could be summed up in single words which includes faith, freedom, and hope.

(Create your own list of positive single words that make you smile or bring you joy, and see for yourself how true his observation is. If you also create a list of words that brings you pain and sorrow, you will see your spirit rise or fall by alternately allowing yourself to be impacted by the words on the two sheets of paper. Given a choice between joy and sadness I choose the joy that uplifting words can bring to my spirit.)

When I need to be inspired toward a new goal, have a desire to lift my spirits, or I just want to contemplate the richness of life, I bring out "My Words of Life" list and drink in the inspiration those words deliver. Every word on the list is positive to me and either expresses something I love or something I want to accomplish.*

In recent weeks I had been searching for a new direction in which to channel my abilities, and I hoped that "My Words of Life" list might inspire me. Recently I had been asking myself on multiple occasions, "What do I want to do at this stage of life?"

I might have continued that thought process, but I knew if I wanted to sleep that night that I had better put away my journal. I decided to meditate and calm my thinking, a genuine challenge for me. Once, I read somewhere that if prayer is when we talk to God, then meditation is when we listen to what God has to say to us. Little did I know that God wanted more than a small conversation with me. Soon my mind calmed, and I quickly fell asleep.

Imagine going from a very deep sleep to wakefulness in the blink of an eye. It happened to me just a short time ago.

Suddenly my spirit slipped out of my body, like a glove pulled from a hand. I had no idea what was happening to me as my spirit lifted away from the bed, circled around my room for a few moments and then flew

---

*I have included "My Words for Life" list in the back of this book in Appendix Two. Create your own list of words upon which you can focus your own growth efforts.

up through my house into the night sky. Was I dying? This separation from my body was simultaneously frightening and thrilling.

When I was a child, on some mornings my father would wake me and say, "Aaron, rise and shine, no one gets off the planet alive, so make every day count."

I guess this might explain my departure from the Earth. According to my father I must have died, and yet I recall that the Apollo 13 astronauts got off the planet alive and returned to tell their story…hmmm.

I couldn't believe it; I was flying away from the Earth at an amazing speed. I looked below me and watched the Earth retreating in the distance while it rotated like a huge blue marble in the blackness of space. How do I describe the glorious feeling of having my spirit soar freely among God's splendid stars?

You should have heard me as I yelled out in excitement, "Oh my God, can it be? I'm flying!" I had often had dreams of flying, like a bird, in the sky, but this was a reality far different than a dream. I felt like a comet shooting through space with the Northern Lights shimmering gold, purple and violet colors around me.

I realized with a jolt that I was flying only because I had left my body behind. Yikes! A shiver ran up and down my spine, I felt like I had just swallowed some electricity.

I should know the feeling, for as a child of three, I stuck an extension cord in my mouth and plugged the other end into a wall socket. I thought that I was creating a microphone, like I had seen at a concert where my father was the bandleader. When the 120 volts rushed in one end of my body my spirit was almost shocked out the other end! After that close brush with death, my mother nicknamed me "Livewire." She said it was because I was overly energized and liked to talk nonstop.

Let me tell you though, flying through space is an even more strange and exhilarating experience than eating electricity. I watched as the miracles of creation were revealed one after another. I wondered what was going to happen next as my mind filled with questions: I was flying away, but where was I going? Was I was really flying? Was I headed to the after-life, that "Great Forever-Ever-Land?" Or was this just a flight of my imag-ination? It had to be more than just imagination. Something was telling me that Heaven was just beyond.

I had often pondered what Heaven might be like. In the past I boasted to my friends that I didn't worry about getting to Heaven because I already had my entry guaranteed. I had been baptized as a child, and the miracle of my own existence was enough to convince me that God him-self existed. After all, how can something come from nothing? I am not talking just about the whole Universe, but even the smallest bit of matter. Sometimes one must go on a journey to discover the right questions, and sometimes one may even stumble on the right answers.

CHAPTER 2

▼

HEAVEN HELP ME

"What on Earth are you doing for Heaven's sake?"

—Anonymous—

As I looked around me I saw other spirits rising from the Earth into the night sky toward a richly colored, shimmering rainbow that had formed over a vast meadow of clouds. I instantly felt a kinship with all of these spirits who had been strangers a moment before.

One of the rising spirits was a girl who I came to know as Sophie. "If the good die young", then that phrase might have been written about this remarkable young woman. She radiated beauty from her spirit, with a positively engaging personality, while those captivating eyes of hers expressed an intense anticipation.

Sophie was the first spirit who I approached as I tried to understand what was happening to me. She put her arm around my shoulder, and with wisdom beyond her years said, "I think we have been called Home to account for our lives."

I looked into her eyes to see if she really believed what she was saying. I swear, I saw Heaven reflected in her eyes, and I just knew she was an angelic soul waiting to be fully realized.

As we passed in awe through the vibrant, spectral colors of the rainbow, I saw an angel bathed in golden light with beckoning arms and open hands.

Just as the angel started to speak, an unbelievable sight distracted our eyes. In the distance, beyond the angel, we could see large open gates and the sunny gardens of what must be Heaven. The rainbow we had passed through, upon our arrival, now stretched as far as the eyes could see over this wondrous place.

Even from a distance Heaven was far more beautiful than anything imagined on Earth. My spiritual heart was pounding with anticipation! Despite all my sins, large and small, Heaven seemed almost within reach.

Sophie and I reacted quickly as we ran past the angel as fast as we could to revel in eternal bliss. I, for one, was expecting all of my afterlife dreams to come true in one fell swoop. Then I noticed something strange: I couldn't fly anymore! If I wanted to get someplace, it required the power of my legs to get me there.

Just as Sophie and I reached the awesome gates of Heaven, they closed! Soon the other spirits joined us at the closed gates.

I quickly glanced to the left and right of the gates and saw a great semi-transparent wall extending as far as my eyes could see. Upon these walls scrolls were spaced every few feet, and they appeared to be just floating in place as if held by invisible nails. Upon each scroll within my view I could see that a message of some sort had been engraved in gold.

Along the wall in both directions I noticed a number of excited spirits passing back and forth through the walls as if they did not exist. The spirits would converse while they walked by the scrolls, as if reading and studying what they found there. After a while they would pass back into Heaven, disappearing behind the wall.

I was tempted to walk along the wall in order to discover the source of the excitement. Then I decided to see if I could simply pass through the walls like the others that I had seen. I reached out my hand and touched the wall near the gate. It was definitely solid and my hand wouldn't pass through. I wondered, "Why can't I enter Heaven?"

Standing next to me were the other spirits who had risen from the Earth, and they were pressed up against Heaven's gates, looking through to the other side. I saw their look of anticipation, bewilderment, and awe, a look that must have registered on my face as well.

I turned aside from the walls to face the majestic Gates of Heaven, masterpieces of design composed of rare woods, precious metals, inlaid mother-of-pearl, and crystals that threw the colors of a rainbow! When I looked closely I saw a delicate design detailing the history of Creation. Sweeping my gaze upward from my bare feet to the sky, I noticed the gates towered in profound splendor to a level far beyond my head.

Imagine that you are standing before these Gates of Heaven, feasting your eyes on the gardens of rare flowers beyond! I held my breath as I listened to music that seemed alive in the air. I also saw the most unusual animals and beautiful birds, like I had never seen on Earth.

Sophie and I were enraptured as we took in the whole scene. We were like two kids with our noses pressed against the bakery counter glass. We could smell the sweet cinnamon in the air, but the hot rolls were just beyond our reach.

I turned to Sophie and said, "What do you think we should do now that the gates are closed and no one is in sight?"

Sophie thought for a moment and replied, "Remember that phrase in the Bible, Aaron? 'Ask, and it will be given you; seek, and you will find; knock, and it will be opened to you.' I can't think of a better time than this to put those words to the test."

So we knocked on the gates and sang out a cheerful, "Hello! Is anybody here? We are the new arrivals, and we are ready and willing to pass through the gates of eternity."

From nowhere an old man approached and announced, "Welcome to these glorious gates! I am the gatekeeper, often called Saint Peter. Do not be surprised by the appearance of these gates or of me. Every soul will see Heaven and its blessed citizenry according to his or her own expectations."

A laugh started to escape from within me, but I resisted the urge to reveal it. Saint Peter was in almost every heavenly joke I had ever heard, and he was always waiting at the "pearly gates."

Now he opened those massive gates, walked out, and stood in front of us with a flowing white beard, glistening in the white radiance of Heaven. He dressed in robes embroidered with gold, looking every bit the wise saint I imagined he should be. Was this real or was it my mind playing tricks on me? "Wakeup if you can," I said to myself, "Wakeup!"

I know that we knocked, and the doors did open for us. We were seeking, and we certainly did find, but something told me that it was going to be more difficult to find what we were really seeking, passage into Heaven. I wondered what would happen next as Saint Peter stood blocking the entrance and prepared to speak to us.

"It's nice to see you at these gates, Sophie. Greetings to you, Aaron, and to all of you, welcome!" Then, Saint Peter said, "I would appreciate it if you would simply call me 'Peter'. We only use first names in the vacinity of Heaven, because to be here you must already have a personal relationship with the Almighty. Next, I would like you to form a line behind Aaron and Sophie so that I might begin to check your qualifications to enter these gates."

Everyone quickly formed into a line of eager souls awaiting our next instructions. Peter then asked a question that I shall never forget:

"May I see your passport to Heaven please?"

I looked at Sophie with wide eyes, and she looked back at me in disbelief as our minds went momentarily blank. Then mental words started to form, "A passport? What kind of passport?" Next I thought, "God must have a great sense of humor if He requests a passport to get into Heaven."

My impulsive nature urged me on; why not use my humor to lighten the gathering drama?

I looked up to Peter and said, "I bet I was supposed to call 1-800-Heaven Help Me, and ask for the heavenly passport special, wasn't I?" I saw no reaction and continued my hopeful, but feeble attempt at comedy.

"Please, don't tell me that they were handing out these passports on one of those Sundays I missed church!" Still getting no reaction, I sensed a deepening crisis. I slapped my forehead, and thought, "Foolish me! That'll teach me to put football before my personal salvation."

Now, I should probably admit here that I never received a good attendance pin for Sunday school, having never attended three weeks in a row. As an adult my sporadic attendance record continued. I do believe, however, that if I had been told that I were earning my Passport to Heaven with excellent attendance, then I might have done much better, or would I? Kind of late to find out now, isn't it Aaron? You sinner you! I thought.

I awaited his reaction and wondered if he noticed my nervous smile. My heart thumped in my chest, as I awaited my fate. I recalled Mark Twain once saying, "If humor isn't allowed in Heaven, you can count me out." Now, I was about to find out what would happen to me and maybe what had happened to that irreverent Mark Twain.

I wondered how St. Peter would respond to my attempt at humor. He didn't keep me waiting for long.

"I know you like football, Aaron," St. Peter chuckled, "…so, I'm sure you'll appreciate that exciting play that utilizes a drop kick. How would you like me to drop kick you out of Heaven until you reach the opposing team?" He paused for effect and then said, "They have never fumbled a kick of mine, and they absolutely refuse to return the ball. Oh yes, they celebrate with a roaring bonfire after the game! Does that get you fired up?"

The most fitting and inappropriate things I might have said at this point were, "Hell? No!" as in "Don't send me to Hell!" and "No, I won't go!" but those words have been misinterpreted. I have often had an irreverent edge to my humor, and the thought did cross my mind that it would be unwise to suggest an alternate play that uses the famous "Hail Mary Pass". I smiled at the thought. My emotions were zigzagging in my brain now. Should I laugh at this point or should I begin crying?

Trying to be wise, I took a more humble approach and asked a few critical questions: "Why am I here, Peter? I'm too young! I haven't even had time for one heart transplant yet! And if that isn't enough help me to understand why any of us need a celestial Passport to enter Heaven?" I stopped talking and for the first time found myself at a loss for words; I was a little shocked, but my mother would have certainly been surprised.

"I don't believe that being at a loss for words is a virtue you often express Aaron," Peter chided as he read my mind. "I will admit, however, that you have a warped sense of humor, but, as you can see, the comedy club entrance is closed!"

"In answer to your first question, we are surprised that you did not arrive here earlier in life. Do you realize how close you came to dying at the ages of 3, 8, 17, 21, 25, 38 and 44?"

I understood what Peter was saying. I had been nearly electrocuted at 3 years of age, had been hit by a car at age 8, had various other vehicle accidents, had fallen through the ice into an Alaskan glacial river at the age of 44, had fallen two stories to the ground from a collapsing ladder, and the list goes on. I had often assumed that I must have had the most fantastic guardian angel.

"With at least seven close calls, Aaron, we thought you were in a hurry to get here. Now it sounds like you want to go back and tempt fate for one last time. Accept the fact that God has a game plan for everyone, and everyone includes you. I should warn you, however, that God does occasionally take someone out of the game either for continued bad performance or because they just choose not to understand the playbook. God has been quite clear about what He expects. Are you His all-star Aaron? I hope so."

"To answer your second question, have you heard the saying, 'Nothing is as constant as change?'"

I nodded my recognition of the adage, and I had the feeling that the other shoe was about to drop and that bad news was on the way.

"Even in Heaven, entry requirements change," Peter said, "There are now over six billion people on planet Earth, and most of you want to get into Heaven. We always have space in Heaven for quality souls, but God has decided that quality standards should be clearly demonstrated. Furthermore, to enter Heaven now, you need a Passport to endorse your accomplishments. It has never been the quantity of souls that counts but the quality. What do you think a quality soul is, Aaron?"

"That is an extremely difficult question," I said. "Let me make a solemn attempt to answer you… I believe a quality soul is one who has compassion for others while actualizing his or her own potential as a human and spiritual being."

"Very good, Aaron. God has many powerful definitions of a quality soul, and your definition certainly celebrates the spirit that God intends. We weren't sure that your early spiritual training took root in you Aaron. Surprise, surprise."

CHAPTER 3

▼

LOST WITHOUT A PASSPORT

"It is good to remember that all the saints in Heaven were once sinners who kept on going."

—*Robert Louis Stevenson*—

Next, Peter explained that every soul had always been tested before entry, but now, having a passport documenting that quality was an added requirement. Then he told us that the passport idea had come from Walt Disney's suggestion to God, "It will insure long lines of seekers!"

I wanted to laugh out loud at the Disney-Passport connection, feeling sure that Peter had to be kidding, however, I remained fearful of being dropkicked into a celebratory bonfire. By the way, to drop kick a football, the ball is dropped toward the foot, and the Hell is kicked out of it. I reached back to see if, as a spirit, I still had a rear that could be kicked!

Of course, all of the other souls had gathered near the gates to hear what Peter would say next in our verbal sparing. I overheard a few spirits saying off-handedly that they hoped that all of the unsuccessful comics like myself would find a warm welcome in Hell!

Wow! Talk about a tough audience. I guess a sense of humor is just something a few of these unlucky souls don't appear to have.

"For those of you seeking The Passport to Heaven," Peter continued, "You will find it a soul searching test. I have faith that the quality souls among you will succeed. If I were you, I would take note of the wisdom along these walls."

Peter opened his arms and pointed to either side of the gates. "Many great souls have their wisdom inscribed here. When God hears a wise phrase that He likes, He adds it immediately. Some souls write their wisdom directly upon the scrolls, and if God agrees, the words are permanently inscribed for the benefit of all."

"On selected scrolls God has identified the creator of the message, and on others he has left the message as anonymous to indicate that many voices have expressed similar words. I could walk outside these walls for eternity and marvel at the truth I see. I am still refreshed and energized by truth and wisdom!"

My ears perked up when he started talking about the truth along the walls. I remembered the spirits who walked in and out of the walls, and now I understood why.

Then I thought of "My Words of Life" list and how refreshing it had been to have my spirit uplifted regularly. I was really interested in what these walls had to say. I wished that I had the time to go around and look upon the walls.

Peter refocused my attention when he said, "Let's get to the matter at hand. I told you earlier that you had to have a Passport to enter these wonderful gates. It is unfortunate that you have reached the gates of Heaven without realizing that a passport is needed."

As Peter said those words I wondered exactly where in Heaven I was supposed to obtain a Passport. I had never seen it written that a passport was required to enter Heaven. Why hadn't someone written a book about it? Of the 70,000 new book titles published each year, not one had informed me about celestial Passports!

"God is a good leader," beamed Peter. "He cares about each of you. He knows how important hope is, and he knows that if you set a high goal and reach it, then your success will be so much sweeter! It is in this spirit that God has directed me to give each of you a chance to solve a riddle. By so doing you will be rewarded."

Peter's comments again reminded me of my parents and all the times I had asked questions that they could not answer. "That's one of the riddles of life," they would say. "Solve that puzzle and you'll be a rich man." Now here was a riddle coming with much more than wealth on the line, of course, being rich in the spirit now had extra meaning.

CHAPTER 4

▼

THE MYSTERIOUS RIDDLE

"Everyone has the opportunity to get a Passport, but God knows everyone
will not realize that they have a Passport in the opportunity."

"Please don't tell me that I have to solve a riddle to get into Heaven!" I
exclaimed. Sure, I expected there might be a final exam, a spirited inter-
rogation, or an even longer confession, but having to solve a riddle now
was like putting all of my brains into a frying pan when they were already
fried. Talk about pressure-cooking!

Saint Peter encouraged us by chuckling, "It's up to each of you, and it
always has been. Think of a diamond. It was just a simple lump of coal
that was transformed under incredible pressure. Are you merely a carbon-
based life form, or are you the jewel that you might become? Rise to the
challenge, and let me see you sparkle!"

See what I mean? Peter started to sound like my dad, "Rise and shine Aaron."
When my parents were still alive I used to love waking to those words because they
were able to deliver them with such spirited enthusiasm. One of my favorite sayings
was, "It's daylight in the swamp and time for all God's creatures to get moving!" I
knew now that I had to get moving in the right direction to get into Heaven.

"Okay, I accept the challenge of the riddle," I said, as if I had any alterna-
tive. Soon all of the other spirits echoed my determination. I guessed that if

the choice was to solve a riddle, or to be dropped kicked from Heaven, the choice was quite clear. "Please. Pleeeeeease! We can really use your help! Where would you suggest we go to obtain a Passport to Heaven?" I implored Peter

"You do give me hope, Aaron," Peter laughed. "I have heard from some recent arrivals that the 'magic words' please and thank you are endangered words on Earth. Don't you love the power of those two words? Understanding people know that these words show humility and respect, encouraging others to be helpful."

"Now, I'm only going to say this once, so listen as if your very afterlife depends upon it," stressed Peter. "Picture the angel who was there to greet you when you first arrived." Our eyes followed his finger pointing off into the distance.

"That angel held a golden opportunity in her outstretched hand, just for the asking! Yet, each of you was so eager to cross into Heaven that you just ignored her offering."

I think we all cleared our throats at the same time when Peter firmly scolded us for our thoughtlessness. He was right, and we were not. Courtesy matters very much, so why did we disregard it?

"Let me put it as plainly as I can to all of you. Everything you do before entering Heaven is a test of your inner quality. Think!" Saint Peter said, "Think! God is looking for souls who represent the quality you find in a rare wood, not the ones who represent the varnish on the wood. We want to find true goodness and wisdom in your soul."

Whenever Peter talked, a rush of memories flooded through my brain. I began to think of all the teachers I had in life, and the best of their wisdom came forward. I felt compelled to review how I had put those words into action. In grade school our teachers told us to treat each other as we wanted to be treated. I could still recall students who I had treated poorly just because they had come from the country and not the city, like me. I felt ashamed of those bad decisions.

It didn't take a genius to figure out Peter's message. We thanked him and ran over the clouds seeking the angel who had the golden opportunity, and the potential solution to the riddle. Peter's words still echoed in my brain, "Everything is a test before entering Heaven." Whoa…deep stuff!

CHAPTER 5

▼

THE ANGEL ISSUES A CHALLENGE

"Think of the diamond. It was just a simple lump of coal that transformed itself under incredible pressure."

—*Anonymous*—

All of us reached the angel at about the same time, and in unison we sincerely apologized for initially having passed her by. The angel lifted her hand. In her fingers she grasped a piece of brilliant white paper. "This paper must be very important," I thought.

She declared, "I do understand the eagerness you must feel over being here, as well as your urgent desire to enter the gates of Heaven. Lately it seems that many souls arriving here are in such a hurry to accomplish everything that they stop thinking about common courtesies."

"My goal presently is to get each of you to pause and think clearly for a minute. I must decide who gets this golden opportunity." she said, "And so, I propose a small challenge."

My thoughts were focused as I pondered, "There is that phrase again, 'golden opportunity', and what did Saint Peter just say about that...Think,

think, think, first a riddle and now a challenge. Where is my stress ball? Or better yet, bring a few buckets of them!"

The angel continued by saying, "I would like each of you to think of a sentence with ten words in it. Each word must have no more than two letters, for a total of twenty letters. This sentence must make sense, must relate to your current predicament, and should suggest who is responsible for the outcome of your life. You have 60 seconds to declare your answer."

60 seconds to answer the greatest challenge of my life! I felt like I was in Final Jeopardy, and I looked around to see if someone like Alex Trebek or Merv Griffin had his hand on the doomsday buzzer.

I thought Heaven was supposed to be a place of rest, but I was becoming more and more exhausted by the moment. I could feel the pressure on me, as a poor lump of coal, and I was hoping a gem would pop out soon.

Where should I start with a challenge like this? In all of my years of school I had never heard of such a sentence. I began to take an inventory of the two letter words I knew: at, to, it, if, we, be, me, is, too… oops to many letters. How many more such words existed? I used to play Scrabble, but I usually didn't get a high point score with just a two-letter word. This sentence also had to express just who was to be responsible for my life. I thought, "Isn't God responsible for my life? But God is a three-letter word…Think Aaron! Think!"

Note to Readers

What sentence would you come up with? Take up to five minutes to think of the answer. Don't read on until you know or give up. If you decide to take two or three days and still can't solve this little challenge, don't despair. I failed miserably myself, as you will see.

Use the remainder of this page or a scrap piece of paper to try and create a sentence that makes sense. A 10-word sentence with a total of 20 letters is an imposing challenge, whether you are on your way to Heaven or anchored to the Earth.

(Yes, this can be done, so take heart.)

I looked around and saw that everyone was deep in thought as we urged ourselves to perform as never before. I felt my anxiety level rising because none of my attempts created a sensible sentence. The angel shook her head back and forth signaling that our "golden opportunity" was quickly slipping away. I could hear the quiz clock ticking in my brain one second at a time: "57, 58, 59, 60, Time is up!"

The angel approached us and asked for our results. Alas! Each of us was informed that our attempts hadn't measured up.

The last soul to try to solve the 10-word sentence was Sophie. When the angel walked up to her she offered two similar sentences with different messages. These were the simple, beautiful, and profound words that she spoke:

"If it is to be,   it is up to me."

After the words were absorbed into our hearts and minds, she astounded us by saying, "While I have accomplished much in my short life, I might have accomplished more with others, had I simply realized another truth."

"If it is to be, it is up to us!"

CHAPTER 6

▼

THE GOLDEN OPPORTUNITY

"An opportunity can be like the air that exists all around us, we know it's there, but we just can't see it."

—*Larry Richardson*—

The truth of Sophie's words felt like cleansing raindrops on my upturned face. We knew that these words were needed on a planet of six billion, a world that was often used and abused in a senseless drive to satisfy personal gain. We thought that in spite of relationship challenges, ignorance, or apathy, it is never too late for individuals to wake up to the ageless truth that working with others accomplishes more than does individual effort.

I was no longer hopeful that I might win, and when my failure tied me for last place with all the other souls, I sighed heavily.

The angel looked over at Sophie, smiled, and said, "The name Sophie is from a Greek word meaning 'wisdom', and you have been true to your name. Did you know that philosophy means 'love of wisdom'?" Sophie's eyes suddenly misted up. She smiled and nodded "Yes."

It must be truly great having a first name that means something special. I wondered what my name, Aaron, meant? For now it looked like my name meant either "late for dinner", or "just plain out of luck".

"You solved the challenge, Sophie, because you understand the importance of personal and shared responsibility in life." Then the angel prepared to hand Sophie the all-important paper that each of us wanted so badly. I watched the angel mysteriously fold the paper three times and she said, "Here it is, your golden opportunity. Make the most of it. Remember your own words, Sophie, if it is to be...."

I waved at Sophie as she started to walk away. I was amazed at how well she had met this challenge. She had truly prepared for the reward the angel had given to her. Yet, I was still mystified. We all needed Passports to get into Heaven but the angel didn't say to Sophie, "Here's your Passport," instead the angel said, "Here is your 'golden opportunity.'" What was the connection between these two concepts? Why call it a golden opportunity when the paper was pure white? Was it merely a figure of speech or something requiring more insight? Finally I tried to remember how the angel folded that paper and why did she fold it that way?

I recall a phrase that my father expressed whenever he saw someone less fortunate than himself, "There but for the grace of God go I." Now, I had seen Sophie walk away, heading toward Heaven. I wished that, "There with the grace of God, I would go."

Reader Instruction #1

The time has come for you to use your sheet of 8½ by 11 inch white paper. You will be shown how the angel used just three folds to create something quite astounding. The diagram that follows visually shows you each step.

Step 1.	The dotted line is a folding line.
Step 2.	The result of folding the top left corner down to the rightside.
Step 3.	The dotted line is another folding line
Step 4.	The result of folding the top right corner down to the leftside
Step 5.	Another dotted folding line.
Step 6.	These are the results from folding the paper in half.

Make sure that your folded paper looks like this.

This is your "golden opportunity"

Place the folded paper on a flat surface in front of you and continue reading the story. More instructions will follow. Do not open the folded paper at this time; just have patience. The best is yet to come!

Illustration #1

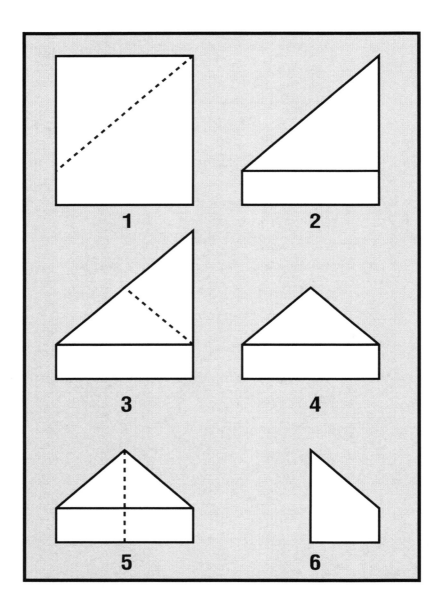

As Sophie turned towards Heaven the angel cautioned her, "Please do not unfold the paper on your way to the gates of Heaven. Saint Peter will ask you for the folded paper, he will open it, and reveal to you what he has found." Calmly, and with a wave, Sophie walked away wishing each of us success in whatever tests lay ahead on our own path to Heaven.

I turned back to the angel and asked for help, "It is very frustrating to get this close and fall so short! Could you pull another opportunity out of your robe as a consolation prize?"

I felt like I had just lost a game show and that the fate of my soul was just decided. In the 1980's I had been on the Family Feud TV Game Show and lost on the final question when I mispronounced the name of the composer, Tchaikovsky. I thanked God that Heaven wasn't on the line back then.

Now that I was near Heaven I hoped that the appearance of being "almost a winner", would stop following me like a shadow.

That stunning angel looked at me and the others with regret in her eyes as she said, "I'm sorry, Aaron, but that was the last opportunity for a Passport to Heaven for the next 1,500 years. As you know, the Passport helps us to ensure that souls are qualified for Heaven, and you'll just have to wait. Sorry."

"The last passport to Heaven for 1,500 years," I thought to myself. "That just can't be! I imagined hearing that the next announcement would be, 'The last stagecoach to Hell is leaving in five minutes, so get in your harness, you sinful slacker, and prepare to pull your weight."

Much to my relief the angel announced, "None of you are destined for Hell unless you make some bad decisions up here. By the way Aaron, what were you thinking regarding passage to Hell?"

I felt a little uncomfortable that my mind was such an open book. "I had better keep my thoughts on a tight leash," I reasoned.

"Use your time near Heaven wisely," she said. "Reflect on your life and the lessons you have learned. Remember this: all of you have lessons to learn if you want to improve the quality of your souls before you enter Heaven. Unleash your potential!"

"Unleash your potential?" Help me Lord! I had thought that my mind was a private place, but now it was opened for inspection and perceptive souls were reading every thought.

CHAPTER 7

▼

WHEN THINGS GO WRONG

"Success is going from one failure to another without losing your enthusiasm."

—*Winston Churchill*—

I listened carefully to the angel as she spoke, hoping that I might learn some little detail that would help me.

"I suggest that those of you who are interested take a walk along Heaven's Great Wall of Wisdom and learn from what you find there."

I asked her, "How it was that the golden scrolls can just float in position along the wall?"

That's when the angel solved a mystery for me. She smiled and said, "Good question, Aaron. The wisdom floats because of the energy in the words. Only phrases uplifting of the spirit will float along those walls."

"I do think wisdom is important," I told the angel, "And I would love to study those walls, but 1,500 years is a long time to study. When I was a freshman at Midland High School in Michigan, it felt like I spent 500 years there in just the first two semesters. But now we are talking about *one thousand five hundred years*!"

The angel paused, restrained a laugh, and then said, "Are you sure that wasn't a reform school you attended? God knows that you could use a little reforming, if it is not too late. Some of your old teachers are up here and they will surely agree."

Ha, ha, ha, I thought, as I looked around at the other unlucky spirits. I saw the spirits drifting away, deep in thought and dejected. These spirits had just given up, but not me! There had to be another door, another way. I was going to find it, even if I had to reform myself!

I attempted to push from my mind the fear of roaming the outskirts of Heaven in a state of limbo, facing an uncertain future. Soon fear broke through my resistance and rushed over my spirit. I asked the angel, "Please help me! What can I do? Isn't there a way for me to get into Heaven sooner rather than later? I have so much to contribute. Give me a chance to earn my wings, or at least a halo! What can I do to prove myself?"

I watched the angel pondering to herself just what to do with a persistent spirit like me. Was everything truly a test? If I gave up too easily, what would that say about my spiritual quality?

I remembered having seen movies about souls earning their wings. Every attempt to become an angel had required overcoming the trials of Job to get the fabled spiritual accessories of a halo, wings, harp, robes and an everlasting peaceful smile. During my earthly existence these treasures of the afterlife didn't get much of my attention, but now they seemed more important than ever.

The angel shook her head and smiled, "Okay, because you won't give up, I'm going to give you another chance to make the grade. Visualize the Great Wall of Wisdom again and imagine what type of wisdom is inscribed there. Share some words of wisdom that have guided your life on Earth. If God hears a phrase that should be added to the Wall, then I shall point you in the right direction."

With a conviction previously not found in my possession, I spoke from my heart and soul inspiring words, which had uplifted my spirit:

"Love doesn't make the world go around, it just makes the ride worthwhile."

"Triumph is nearest when defeat seems inescapable."

"There are two ways to spread the light: be a candle or the mirror that reflects it."

"Good people are good because they've come to their wisdom through failure."

"Have faith. When things go wrong, don't you dare go with them!"

The angel pointed at me saying, "That's a phrase that celebrates the inspiring wisdom on the wall."

"Have faith. When things go wrong, don't you dare go with them!"

"Your faith and persistence may yet set you free, Aaron. I have risked my reputation for other promising spirits, but I soon found that many spirits just don't want to take the time to understand the wisdom all around them."

"I know what you mean," I said. "I might have saved a lot of hassles in my life if I had just listened more to the wisdom of my parents, teachers and friends. Why is it that people often do not want to learn from the mistakes of others?"

"One of God's more humorous souls up here," said the angel, "is Mark Twain who answered that question, by saying, 'When I was 17 years old I was shocked at how stupid my parents were. When I turned 21 years old, I was amazed at how much they had learned in a few short years.' People think they know everything especially when they are young," the angel lamented, "It is fortunate that, with age, wisdom has a chance to grow. We should never stop learning."

It was a relief to hear the angel say that Mark Twain had made it to Heaven. At times he had been very irreverent, and yet, he had made it! Alas, maybe there was still hope for me.

Chapter 8

▼

Friendship Matters

"Sharing what you have is far more important than what you have."

—*Albert M. Wells Jr.*—

"I promised to point you in the right direction, but your trials are not yet over, Aaron. You will soon have the chance to put your words into action. The angel put her arm around my shoulders, leaned over, and said to me, "Run after Sophie and see if you can convince her, as a friend, to share a portion of her 'golden opportunity' with you. It just might be your 'golden opportunity' as well. If you do catch up to her please tell her something for me." Then the angel leaned down and whispered the message in my ear and added, "Godspeed Aaron!"

I thanked the angel for coming to my rescue and ran through the clouds while pondering her message. Soon I was breathless and exhausted, but I was enthusiastic to make my appeal to Sophie's heart and soul.

As the reader, you may now be asking how a spirit could be out of breath and exhausted. I asked an angel that question later, and the angel laughed and said, "Your spirit must be flabby! Everyone knows that the door to Heaven sometimes doesn't open for the flabby spirit."

I felt embarrassed by the nugget of truth just awarded to me. "Flabby spirit," huh? If it's flabby, maybe I do need to strengthen it with a long walk around that Wall of Wisdom someday and someday might have to be today. One, two, three, four, strengthen the spirit and open the door…one, two, three, four.

Thankfully, I reached Sophie just before she made it to the gates of Heaven.

"Sophie, please listen to me!" I pleaded. I was gulping air in an effort to say the words that might save me. As she turned to me, I took a deep breath and told her, "The angel asked me to give you this message. 'If you help someone to get their own boat across a river, then your boat will surely cross to the far shore.'"

Sophie listened carefully as she contemplated my message. I could sense the connections being made in her mind as she searched for the depth of meaning that those words might contain.

"Sophie, I believe the angel was saying that if you can help me to cross into Heaven, then I in some way would be helping you to cross into Heaven too. I don't quite understand, but I think it has something to do with that mysterious riddle that we were supposed to solve."

"The angel gave you what they call a 'golden opportunity', but where is this Passport they keep talking about? Whatever that angel handed to you is in some way the key to the riddle."

Poets have said that the eyes are the windows to the soul. I looked into Sophie's eyes as she looked into mine, and I tried to convey the urgency of my plea and its potential importance to her.

"Please, consider my next question very carefully. Believe me when I say that I will understand if you have to say, no!" I paused for a moment and then asked for her to make the most incredible sacrifice of her life, "Would you be willing to share a portion of your paper with me?"

It made me heartsick to present Sophie with such a difficult dilemma. It appeared that she had nothing to lose by just walking through the gates, but, possibly, everything to lose if she helped me. She had been awarded the "opportunity" because of her wisdom, but if she tore this paper apart now, she might destroy her only chance to get into Heaven. I knew in my heart that if she was refused entry because of something I did, then I would have to refuse to walk into Heaven if given the chance, and I would return every piece of paper to her.

I saw Sophie close her eyes and ask God for the "Wisdom of Solomon" to do the right thing.

I remember reading in the Bible that King Solomon suggested a child be divided between two women who each claimed it for her own. The real mother decided to give up the baby instead of splitting it asunder and was rewarded with possession of her child.

To split? or not to split? To give? or not to give? It is the same decision that I have faced at many of the crossroads in my life.

Suddenly a smile lit up Sophie's face as she held the folded paper in one of her hands and carefully tore away one third of it. She dropped the miscellaneous pieces into my waiting hands. What a gift! I thought about how she had actually shared her opportunity with someone she had only known for a brief period, me!

"Aaron, I have only known you a short time but I believe that you are a good man. I do have a great faith in you, and I feel that what I am sharing with you will make a difference. When I was in middle school, I remember that we had a food drive for the hungry in Los Angeles. Each day I brought food to the school and gave up some of my lunch money. Somehow I knew inside of me that my small contribution would make a big difference. We will both need our faith, Aaron."

Reader Instruction and Illustration #2

Please pick up the folded paper that you created earlier in reader instruction #1. Choose one of the two following diagrams, depending on whether you are right-handed or left-handed. Your folded paper should match the general appearance of *one* of these two drawings. **The two views are shown so as to make cutting easier.**

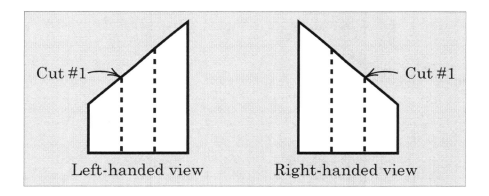

Please look at the diagram on this page and use a pair of scissors, (scissors work best), or tear very carefully. You will be cutting just *1/3* of the paper away at this time in the story.

Cut along the imaginary line (#1) as shown above from bottom to top completely, or if you are tearing the sheet tear straight slowly from top to bottom along the line (#1).

Place the pieces that you cut or tear off down on a table or flat surface and be careful **not to lose any of these pieces**. These represent the pieces of paper that Sophie just shared with Aaron.

I looked to see the torn pieces that Sophie had placed in my hand. I felt grateful and told her so! What happened next I couldn't explain. Something inside of me urged me, in a most insistent voice, to ask for even more help and to use my humor as a tool.

Sophie was looking at her folded paper and probably wondering if she had done the right thing by tearing some away.

So, with a touch of humor, I said to Sophie, "I believe that I am a fairly good person. In fact, I am probably as close to sainthood as I shall ever be, which really doesn't mean that I am very close at all." Then I held my arms wide apart.

Sophie laughed, putting her hand to her mouth to muffle the expression of humorous disbelief at my alleged sainthood.

I continued by telling her, "Surely my sins weigh more then the pieces of paper in my hand." I held my hands out in a begging maneuver.

She laughed again and said, "Only God knows, Aaron, if you are a compulsive sinner or a lover of truth. I can't believe that God would send a good person like you to limbo. Your trials must have a purpose beyond your understanding. Don't be afraid to ask for help Aaron."

Sophie had a special way of making me look at something in a different perspective as I opened my hands and inspected her gift of paper to me.

"I'm afraid that I might need more than this in order to get into Heaven." I hesitantly held out my hands to let her see what she had given me.

Once again Sophie thought. She smiled and ripped off half of her remaining folded paper, handing those pieces to me, too.

I couldn't believe her generosity. Ernest Hemmingway had once said, "Courage is grace under pressure." Perhaps he had a person like Sophie in mind when he penned those words.

Of course, there are usually at least two ways to look at things, and I remember a funny phrase by Marvin Kitman who said, "If God wanted us to have courage, why did he give us legs?" When to have courage, is one of those big questions.

Perhaps it is helpful that near Heaven there is no place to which one might run, neither undeservedly through the gates into Heaven, or back to Earth. So, if one has much courage, this is the place to demonstrate it.

My courage to face adversity had been tested many times on Earth, and I recalled, a saying of Confucius that our greatest glory is not in ever having fallen, but in rising every time we do fall. I was beginning to understand that the wisdom I appreciated on Earth and now recalled had some eternal value.

Reader Instruction and Illustration #3

Now look at the diagram on this page and cut with scissors or carefully tear along dotted line (#2) as shown. The original paper is reduced in size as parts are shared.

Place the new pieces with the first pile of pieces that you removed earlier in direction #2. Again, be careful not to lose **any** of these pieces...Saint Peter would frown on this, and he would probably say, "It's not wise to lose the peace that brings you your salvation."

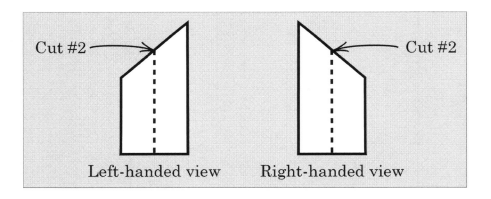

Left-handed view   Right-handed view

Remember that the two different views are just meant as an aid to cutting the paper; depending upon what hand you use to cut the paper.

CHAPTER 9

▼

SEEING IS BELIEVING!

"The time is always right to do what is right."

—*Martin Luther King, Jr.*—

After sharing parts of her precious paper, Sophie turned back toward Heaven and knocked on the gates. Once again she was enthralled with the view as she waited for Peter to approach from the distance. I prayed silently that her gift to me would not jeopardize her entry into Heaven. Sophie now held in her hand only a third of the paper that the angel had originally given to her.

I hoped that the words of Martin Luther King, Jr. from the 1960's would ring true for the sharing that had just taken place outside the gates of Heaven. "The time is always right to do what right." But were we right to share and divide the paper?

Peter approached Sophie, and his face lit up with a smile that radiated goodwill as he asked her the big question:

"May I see your Passport to Heaven please?"

Reaching out, he carefully took the remaining paper from her offering hand. "Let's see what we have here." Slowly he unfolded the paper and held it up for Sophie to see.

I gasped at what Peter revealed and noticed a tear of joy and thankfulness in Sophie's eye. I wouldn't have believed it had I not seen it for myself. I would guess that most of us have a little bit of a doubting Thomas in us. I am sure my face registered surprise and awe at the revelation which the paper presented. I was impressed.

How was it possible for a single piece of paper to be folded in such a way as to create the Passport to Heaven after it had been torn into pieces? Was there a hidden message being delivered that I needed to interpret?

Suddenly I understood the connection between the 'golden opportunity,' and the Passport to Heaven. An opportunity is nothing unless one takes action and makes something out of it. Sophie solved her riddle by willingly sharing her gift, but what was going to happen to me? What action would be required of me with a handful of paper pieces? What did I have to share? The questions were racing through my mind like the rushing waters of a steep mountain stream.

Reader Instruction and Illustration #4

At this time take the largest single folded piece of paper, which is noted in the diagram below. This is the piece that Sophie had left after sharing the other 2/3 of her opportunity and is the paper that she presented to Peter.

Slowly unfold your paper to reveal what brought such a big smile to Peter and a gasp to my lips. It is " **The Passport To Heaven.**"

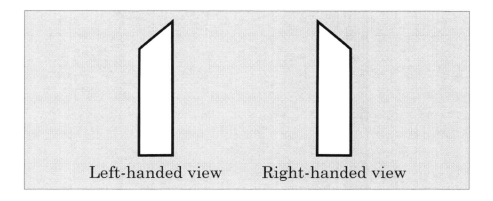

Left-handed view   Right-handed view

Please unfold your paper before continuing on

Saint Peter was obviously overjoyed as he boomed, "Well done, Sophie, my child! You have not disappointed us. Your compassionate life and your sharing soul are indeed a wonderful gift for God today. It is refreshing to have you here in Heaven."

I watched as Peter hugged Sophie while her arms gently returned his embrace. "Do you realize, Sophie that you have solved the riddle that God gave to you? By sharing your 'golden opportunity' you turned something common into something very special, your Passport to Heaven. Welcome, Sophie," Peter said. "Your family, friends, and even Philo have been awaiting you."

The gates slowly opened and a small dog with black button eyes and white fluffy fur ran up to greet Sophie. He licked her hand in recognition and shook joyfully as she lifted him.

I remembered earlier when the angel talked about the meaning of the word philosophy and Sophie's eyes had started to water. Now I knew why. **Philo** is the Greek word for "love" and, of course, **Sophie** is the Greek word for "wisdom."

I was so touched by the scene unfolding before me that I felt a poetic verse forming. Suddenly, to my left I saw the words in my thoughts appear on a golden scroll floating near the gates.

> *Open your spiritual eyes and see*
> *that wisdom and love*
> *are meant to be.*
> *Discover what is true*
> *each and every day,*
> *by letting wisdom and love*
> *show you the way."*

I remembered my Mom having once said, "Why, Aaron, you're a poet, and I didn't know it." My brothers would have asked me what I did with the money I supposedly spent on poetry lessons. Some memories surely bring a smile to one's face and warmth to the heart!

Sophie waved back at me as she crossed the threshold of Heaven and wished me well in whatever might yet lie ahead for me.

"Thank you for helping me to cross the threshold," she said. "I am praying that when your moment comes you will cross it too. By the way!" she shouted. "Remember those words on the scroll just to the right of the gate. Look to the right of the gate!"

CHAPTER 10

▼

BAD NEWS, GOOD NEWS

"The greater the difficulty the more glory you achieve in surmounting it."

—Epicurus—

As Sophie walked into the distance beyond the trees I lost sight of her. Then I looked closely at the scroll to the right of the gate. I recognized the message as one of the shortest most powerful speeches in history.

Winston Churchill gave one of the great speeches of his life before a military academy in England years after World War II. He was asked to give an inspirational address about his success in the war to a graduating class of cadets.

Churchill stood up, walked to the center of the stage, and said, "Never, never, never, never, ever give up!" Churchill then sat down to stunned silence and then thunderous applause as his powerful words seeped into the hearts and minds of everyone present.

Churchill's words were ringing in my head as I approached Peter again. In my hand I held an assortment of pieces of paper. I also held an uncertain feeling in my heart about what was about to happen. I thought back to that book titled: *"When Bad Things Happen to Good People,"* by Harold

Kushner. I wondered if I might become a new chapter in some future revised edition.

What should I do? I felt the wrinkles deepening on my forehead as I ran my hands through my hair. I wondered if St. Peter would laugh me off the playing field when I handed him a bunch of paper pieces that looked like confetti. I recalled how amazed I had been by what Sophie had given Peter and I wondered if I would be amazed twice in the same day.

I remembered when my daughter was a child, I would watch her study bugs on the sidewalk. Whether the bugs were alive or not, she was still amazed by the creatures. One of the great things about having children is the ability to rediscover the simple and wondrous pleasures of life in everyday happenings. There seems to be an expectation in children for what the new day will bring, I chose then to honor that expectation.

When it looks as if all is lost, I find that I need to remember that the future is yet to arrive. With appropriate actions, situations can be changed for the better in an instant!

Reader Instruction #5

Gather all of the small pieces of paper that you tore or cut from your original folded paper. Place them in one of your hands.

These pieces were all that remained for me to hand over to Saint Peter.

Imagine that Sophie handed these pieces to you and how bewildered you might be to present mere scraps of paper to Saint Peter. Can something special again be made from almost nothing?

My heart was pounding as I approached St. Peter. I felt like I was going to the office of the IRS to be audited, and I wasn't sure what was about to happen. Finally I walked up to the gate and stood in front of him."

True to his past actions, Peter held out his hand and asked me the big question:

"May I see your Passport to Heaven please?"

As I put all of the pieces of paper in his hand I was concerned that he wasn't smiling as he had for Sophie, and yet, he did have an unexpected look of anticipation on his face. I decided to plead my case that it hadn't been my intention to come to Heaven so unprepared. I had not expected to die so young nor so quickly, and the need for a Passport was news to me.

I felt silly begging for my salvation, but my heart said, "Pride be damned! Beg, you fool!"

"Let's just see what we have here," he pondered aloud as he stroked his beard. "I can tell you now, Aaron, that your future will be spelled out in these pieces of paper you have given me." Slowly he began to unfold each piece of paper, one at a time.

As for me, I felt like a fool because it appeared that I had just given him a handful of confetti. It was almost like saying, "Here are all of my sins. Here are the pieces of my life, my dreams, and my regrets. Now, what will you make of that?"

Peter continued to rotate the pieces of paper until a word suddenly materialized out of the chaos. As he pulled his hands back, I saw the shocking result. My mouth dropped open again, and I just about fainted on the spot.

I didn't realize it at the time, but I was about to be taught a valuable lesson as useful in life as in Heaven. The lesson I learned was: Things are often not as bad as they first appear. However, I can understand why I was not too optimistic with the result of the word created by Peter. After all, what word can be worse?

I started to chant the word "faith" over and over in my mind. "Faith! Faith! I must have faith!" I was reminded of the 1960's phrase that helped to instill hope, "Keep the faith, baby!" Here was a perfect example of how I cope, "When under stress, look for inspiration from the past, and try to put things in a better perspective!"

Reader Instruction #6 with Illustration #5

Open all eight of the smaller pieces that you cut from the original paper. As you open the pieces of paper lay them on a flat surface and see if you can spell out a word. Your unfolded pieces of paper should appear like the shapes in the following diagram.

If you discover the word or you are ready to move on to the next step, please continue.

Reader Instruction #7 with Illustration #6

In the following diagram you may observe how Saint Peter placed these eight pieces of paper to spell out the word HELL. You should have opened your pieces of paper and placed them similarly. If you haven't spelled out the word HELL yet, then please do so now. In fact, you may have discovered other words, but more about that later.

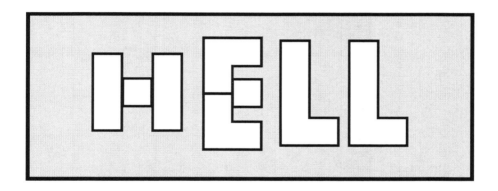

Well, it looks like you have been sent to HELL. This may amuse some readers and others may be concerned about what this might mean for them. If you were to share just what you have learned so far you would be sending other people to HELL.

For those hoping for a better outcome for themselves and others, please read on. This story gets stranger yet.

At this moment of my imagined doom I looked past St. Peter, through the gates of Heaven, and mentally pleaded with God. "Oh, God! What did I do to deserve this? Do you really think that I deserve to go to Hell? Save me from this fate, and I will do whatever you ask, within reason!" I think somewhere in the deep recesses of my soul I knew that I would be in a situation like this one day, so I added "within reason" to hedge my bets. What if God said be a hermit, or roam the desert for 40 years. Then again should anyone refuse God?

As you read this story you may be thinking that this kind of a "God promise", made at times of great peril, sounds familiar. Be truthful now, haven't you made this promise, once or twice in your life, perhaps when you were flying in an airplane and it hit an air pocket? After the danger was over did your promise just sort of evaporate?

With all of the mental concentration I could muster I thought, "Work for me now, promise-of-promises!"

I turned to Peter and said, "This must be a mistake!" Peter looked back through the gates of Heaven, and there was God looking at him! They both smiled.

Peter must have been reading my thoughts again, because, he said, "Yes, you are seeing God, you fortunate soul!"

"Most people don't realize that they are seeing God every day of their lives, but they don't recognize the face: in nature, in others, and in all the wonders of life. Think about that statement when you have a chance, Aaron, and let the truth set you free," Peter announced.

I thought about those wise words and they gave me hope.

Peter reminded me that Sophie had solved the riddle of "The Passport to Heaven," and she was home. But I had not yet solved the riddle.

"Remember," Peter advised, "Every problem contains the seed of its own solution, even if you can't see it at this moment. And undoubtedly you've heard the old saying, 'When life gives you a bunch of lemons either make some lemonade or learn to juggle the fruit as fast as you can.'"

"Why am I getting such a bunch of wise sayings?" I wondered when what I really needed were answers. Suddenly I wished that I were back in school so that I could look at somebody else's test paper. Oops! Chalk one more old sin up on the board for God's review.

Reader Instruction #8

Take a moment and think about what you would do. In my moment of greatest disappointment I was about to find a solution that would let me cross into Heaven. Remember the riddle that St. Peter gave me to solve earlier in this book:

"Everyone has the opportunity to get a Passport to Heaven, but most people will never realize that they have a Passport in the opportunity."

Do you recall that Sophie only discovered her Passport to Heaven by sharing her opportunity with me? Throughout this story I have shared those same pieces with you. Let me give you a hint. Is it possible to find your own Passport in the opportunity before you? I did. If you want to attempt to solve this riddle, take a few moments before proceeding. My solution will be revealed on further on in this book.

CHAPTER 11

▼

THE LAST PASSPORT TO HEAVEN

"Triumph often is nearest when defeat seems inescapable."

—B.C. Forbes—

I looked at the pieces of paper once, and I looked at them again and again. I thought about how they reminded me of other challenging times in my life. I thought of times when my life seemed to fall into pieces and other times when I brought the pieces together again.

Often it was hope that gave me the courage to work on the changes needed in my life. I believe that hope uplifts the spirit. If hope has its foundation rooted in reality, then it is one of the last things that a person should ever choose to lose.

Now I was staring Hell in the face with both hope and discouragement. "Why can't I solve this riddle?" Repeatedly that thought came to mind. Then I threw my hands up in despair and said, "I can't do this! Who cares if giving up might be another sin to put up on the old chalkboard."

You may be wondering what this chalkboard of sin is. When I was a teen my dad mentioned over breakfast one morning that he had a strange dream about me during the night, and he wanted to share it.

In that dream my dad recalled that he had died and approached a stairway leading to Heaven. At the bottom of the stairs he was handed a piece of chalk by an angel who told him to climb up the stairs until he reached the chalkboard at the top. When he got there he was supposed to write down every sin that he had ever committed while Saint Peter looked on. When he got halfway up this long staircase he saw me, hurrying back down the other way. My father asked, 'Aaron where are you going?' I replied, 'I'm going back to get two more cases of chalk dad!'"

I remember laughing and choking on my cereal at the same time the milk was running out of my nose. I was sure that this joke was a lesson for me about being a better teenager. He must have surmised that I was sinning on a regular basis as girls began to enter and leave my life. I like recalling my dad's sense of humor. However, I must get back to my present situation.

Suddenly far below me I heard my name shouted, "Aaron! Did you call me? You did say you were giving up on Heaven didn't you?"

Now the hair stood up on the back of my neck as I heard devilish laughing. Soon my nose alerted me to the hellish odor of sulfur in the air. I didn't have to be told that the Devil was calling me, and I shivered as if someone had just walked across my grave.

The sales pitch of the Devil was coming and I had seen enough movies to know that when you make a deal with this guy, it never turns out to be good. So, I surely wasn't surprised when I heard the Devil say, in a slick and fast-talking salesman tone, "It's that hopeless riddle isn't it? Why not just give up and come to Hell instead? Our philosophy down here is simple, 'When you sin you grin! If you snooze you lose.' Am I coming in loud and clear, Aaron?"

Of course he was coming in loud and clear! I thought about the times I had sinned and grinned, and yet, there had always been a price to pay somewhere down the road.

"Don't put up with the struggles that God throws at you!" The Devil continued, "No tests, no riddles, and no exams are conducted in Hell! Every vice that you desire, and even more, awaits you here. Everybody can smoke in Hell! Every moment is a gamble! And we don't even serve water here, just alcohol. Aaron, you always light up a room with your wit and charm, come join us! Believe me! Your spirit will never burn brighter than in Hell. Stand up and be counted, are you a man or a marshmallow?"

Now, in a moment of weakness, from so many recent trials, this offer of fun and games seemed almost good, but I recalled what Peter had said, "Everything before entering Heaven is a test." Besides, I wondered, what does the Devil do with marshmallows in Hell? Does the phrase, 'crispy anyone,' grab you?

"As you think, so you are, and as you choose, so you will be." Henry James, put it very clearly.

I recalled reading in the Bible that Christ faced a relentless list of temptations from the Devil in the wilderness and resisted them all. I knew that I too must choose what is good and what is true. I shouted as I shut my ears to the Devil, "I don't consider Hell to be an option, don't want it, never will, no how, and no way! If the Kingdom of God is within me as Christ promised, then the solution must also be within me, and I will find it!"

I dismantled the word HELL and the negativity that it represented. Then I began to rotate the pieces while looking into my heart for a clue. As if by inspiration, I saw the solution in Sophie's farewell words to me. My moment had finally come, and it was time to cross over the threshold. Why hadn't I seen the obvious?

Final opportunity to figure out "The Last Passport to Heaven."

Reader Instruction #9 with Illustration #7

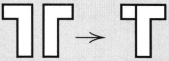

Step #1 - Overlap the two L pieces as shown.

Step #2 - Overlap the two E pieces as shown.

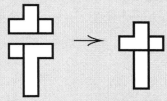

Step #3 - Overlap step #1 and step #2 as shown.

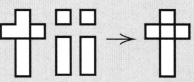

Step #4 - Place the remaining pieces on the cross.

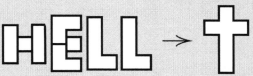

The transformation from doom to glory is complete.
The solution was available all along.

CHAPTER 12

▼

I CHOOSE YOU!

"Don't leave before the miracle happens."

—Anonymous—

"Well done, Aaron," Peter said with a laugh as he looked over my shoulder. "Guess what happens now?" I hoped that that was just a rhetorical question, since I felt as if I had finally earned my entrance to Heaven. I saw Peter smile as he announced, "This is where I do the "Hail Mary Pass" you were thinking of earlier. Your family and friends will try to catch you in the end zone of Heaven. If they catch you, then you are in. If they drop you, well…"

Peter looked at me with a twinkle in his eye, and let me see, that once again, he had known my thoughts all along. "It's okay to laugh now, Aaron," he said. "We really do have a great appreciation for humor up here." By the way, Aaron, you were thinking earlier that it would be nice if your name meant something special. Well, it certainly does. Aaron is a wonderful Hebrew name meaning 'Enlightened One.'"

I was overflowing with relief at Peter's humor and kind words, and my face beamed, as I prepared to cross into Heaven. And yet, I hesitated, wondering how I might share my knowledge with the souls who still needed to cross through these gates. I felt Peter's hand on my shoulder as he gently urged me to cross over.

I saw souls of family and friends, and souls of people about whom I had only read. I quickly hugged my parents as I was surrounded in love and congratulated on my new mission of sharing. "What new mission?" I said in disbelief! "I just got here. I wish to find my wings, adjust my halo, play my harp, and walk the golden streets. I would like to talk to my parents, hug my grandparents, and see the wonders of Heaven! I wish to ask God every previously unanswerable question that has ever crossed my mind. Am I asking too much?"

Somehow they had all heard my promise to God that I would do whatever He wanted if He spared me from the torments of Hell.

Suddenly, God was standing next to me! In a comforting voice He said, "Aaron, don't be afraid. I am appearing to you now in a form that you can understand so that you will not simply faint dead away. Nod if you are hearing me earthling."

I was more than humbled to be in the presence of God. Slowly, I nodded my head, proving to Him that I wasn't catatonic. "Aaron, I want you to return to Earth. Share the wisdom that you have seen on the walls of Heaven as well as the message about the 'Last Passport to Heaven.' I remember you saying that someone should write a book about this. I choose you!"

Somehow I knew that he was reading every thought in my mind, so I tried to think good, clear, and squeaky-clean thoughts.

God smiled and said, "Relax, Aaron, you have many questions that you would like to ask Me, don't you?" I just nodded, and He said, "For now, you may ask three questions about what you have just experienced, and I will gladly answer them. If you have other questions about how and why I created the universe, how big Heaven is, or about My existence, and so on, they must await answers until you return from your mission. And don't worry, you will eventually return. Do we have an understanding?"

I was about to answer, but He continued, "Oh, by the way, I have a little advice. Try not to preach too much when you share what I am about
to tell you. Sometimes people don't want to hear what I have to say, and
they will turn off their invisible hearing aids.

Simply write what I am inspiring you to write, and then move on.
People will only learn when they are ready to learn. Those ten little words
are very powerful, aren't they?"

People will only learn when they are ready to learn.

I thought about those words and how, in my own life, I had put off
learning such important lessons. I believe at times we aren't ready to learn
because our wisdom hasn't matured enough. I often wished that God
would send someone down to Earth every few years to set the record
straight. I imagined that this messenger from God would give us a common wisdom that people of all ages would adopt and put into action
immediately.

"Aaron, please remember that all of your thoughts are coming at me like
meteors. I won't be able to respond to all of them, but I will respond to that
last thought. Millions of people look up to Heaven every day and wonder
why I don't send someone down to Earth to clean house. When will they
learn that I sent each of you to make Earth a better place! Each of you has
a wonderful and unique contribution to make. You were my messenger."

Just then, I remembered that I had heard such an idea, 'on Earth and
in Heaven' but had not really grasped the greatness of the words. I recalled
that, 'If it is to be, it is up to me,' and 'it is up to us.'

"Finally," God said, "When I am sharing with you listen carefully to
what I am telling you. I will answer your three questions at a level that I
believe you will understand. Ask each question and wait for My complete
answer please."

If God spoke to you and said, "I need you to do something for Me."
What would you do? Of course, I accepted the mission immediately, and

I should say, without reservations. I also quickly agreed that I would only ask three questions.

Believing that I should recognize an opportunity when I see it, I found the chance to return to Earth again too hard to pass up. Just the thought of returning was making me homesick for friends, relatives, and the wonderful opportunities that life on Earth has for each of us.

Some say that the real purpose in life is to have a purpose, and now I clearly had that. I knew that I should tell the story of "The Last Passport to Heaven" with its wise message of sharing and love. I should reveal that the Passport offers an inclusive embrace to all who wisely use it.

I also knew that if I was going to be effective at accomplishing my mission, I had better get a few answers to some important questions that enquiring minds on Earth might ask of me. I looked up at God and said in my most respectful and appreciative voice, "Here are my three questions."

Question #1…Is there only one True Faith that earns a soul the right to pass through the gates of Heaven?

"Great question, Aaron! Do you think that others are able to accept the truth? My words have been interpreted in many ways on Earth so that people become even more confused at times. Just because one person expresses My words differently than another, or calls Me by a different name, does not mean the words are to be discounted or held as worthless and untrue. If you want to see to what degree I am embraced by a particular faith or belief, look for these qualities of truth:

> Does the faith or belief have a foundation rooted in the Golden Rule? Do unto others, as you would have them do unto you.

> Are love, goodness, mercy, caring, sharing and charity expressed in the literature and actions of the group?

Are individuals encouraged to personally develop and to help others develop toward their highest potentials of good?

Are members of a faith understanding and tolerant of others with different beliefs?

Do the members believe that positive and compassionate service to others is a great virtue of mankind?

Finally, do they believe in a power and creative force larger than themselves that has gifted them with life?

I could go on and on with this particular answer, but people, as I said earlier, don't like too much preaching even when it comes from Me.

It is regretful that many individuals refuse to see the light until they see My light here. Some sorry souls will remain here, briefly, only to find out that I have for now turned the lights out for them. I have created all that is. Repeatedly, I have shared a positive vision proclaimed by many teachers on Earth. You can help others to find and embrace the common ground of truth underlying positive faiths. Each person must grow to see this truth for him or herself, but a little inspiration never hurts.

People must realize that what they sow shall soon be revealed in the quality of the harvest. Love brings love. Hate brings hate. You sow what you reap. How can I say it any plainer than that?"

Question # 2…The Passport is such an amazing creation. I would like to know if all of its wonders have been revealed to me?

"I shall briefly answer a question that you have thought about but have not asked. Not every soul will go through the trails and tribulations that I have put you through. I needed someone for a mission, and I needed to know that you would persevere and express My wisdom as a teacher. I also wanted a book written and I needed to know that you would follow through.

Now, regarding your question about the Passport. I can see that you really do enjoy being amazed by the simplest aspects of life, and that says much about the vitality of your spirit. You saw a cross in the paper, and you were awed. You saw the word HELL in the paper, and you were shocked. Other souls have created the words: Soul, Love, Sin, Lies and so on. Sophie just shared two parts of her Passport. Some souls have shared their Passports with ten cuttings of the same paper and produced words like "Salvation", "Jesus", or "Faith", and even longer words can be created.

Even I can be brought to tears, Aaron, by what some souls can create from their own life, or a simple piece of paper. I remember two brothers who had perished in an automobile accident in Mexico. These two brothers, Juan and Miguel, loved Truth and lived their faith everyday by helping others less fortunate than themselves.

The brothers came to these gates and shared one "Golden Opportunity" between them. I saw them cut the paper in a unique way and hand it to Peter. When Peter opened up the paper, he and I saw that Juan and Miguel had created the three crosses of the crucifixion, all connected at the bottom. The pieces that had been cut away earlier now completed the two crosses at each side of the main cross when they were added back. Can you even imagine the impact that had on me?*

Experiment with "The Passport to Heaven", Aaron, and encourage your readers to do the same. Everyone must find the Truth for him or herself. I inspired the creation of 'The Passport to Heaven', and it demonstrates many lessons I wish to have taught on Earth. I intended this simple little piece of paper to capture the imagination of people and to open their hearts and minds to creatively express My Truths. Now, question number three, please."

---

* At the end of this book I have included an illustration that shows you how to create the "Way of the Three Crosses" in Appendix Three.

Question # 3…Will people believe me when I say that they will need a Passport to get into Heaven?

God started to laugh, and the tears were soon rolling down his cheeks. "Aaron, Aaron, Aaron, the Passport is merely a symbol of your true soul, the real you. All people are born with the 'golden opportunity' to be quality people and to develop quality spirits. The Passport to Heaven is only intended to be an instructive parable."

"I have said it over and over since people could first understand that I was speaking to them. Everyone must find out My Truths within his or her own life and decide what paths are to be taken. Each makes a multitude of decisions offering opportunities to realize those Truths."

"I won't cover all of the conditions that each soul on Earth might encounter during their life, Aaron, but I want you to know that I am aware of all the trials and tribulations that each soul experiences. People have highs and lows, are healthy or ill, are free or enslaved, are empowered or held down. And yet, their souls will speak out."

"I would like you to title your book 'The Last Passport to Heaven.' The last and only Passport a person will get is the quality of his or her own soul."

"I know the potential for quality of each and every soul. I take the essence of an individual into consideration in determining final rewards. Each person makes his or her own Passport"

"People will see in your book what they choose to see. Some may just see a simple exercise in paper cutting. Others will see the deep meaning in the words you share. So just get used to their different responses. I have done so for thousands of years, and occasionally I still have to shake my head in disbelief."

Before I was allowed to leave Heaven, God suggested that I walk along the Great Wall of Wisdom and record the messages I saw. He recommended I sprinkle these truths throughout my book, like gold dust, to be discovered and appreciated.

He also said, "The messages should uplift the spirits of your readers, providing guidance to help them achieve success." Then, God smiled at me, turned away, and walked into the gardens of Heaven radiating his love in all directions. As I watched Him fade away into the distance He gave me a farewell wave over His back.

I have read in ancient literature that to look directly upon God when He is speaking may induce blindness. I noticed in Heaven the eyes of spirit need not be blinded.

I have seen that God appears in any manner that He chooses, and that He can have whatever impact He desires upon a person or soul to whom He is talking.

It seemed like I walked for hours along those energizing walls, and I recorded all that I saw in my heart and mind. Finally, I arrived at a blank scroll near the gate. I saw a pen with gold ink, and I somehow just knew that God wanted me to add a few words of my own to the scroll on the wall.

So, I began to write the words that I sensed within, "The Passport to Heaven is created through the realization of God's great Truths. 'Golden opportunity' is found in every moment. By choosing to express His Truths in our lives, the gates of Heaven are opened!" Once those words had been written on the scroll, I felt a gentle, invisible tug, as I was pulled away from Heaven.

Suddenly, like an astronaut on an overstretched silver tether, I felt myself gaining speed and watched Heaven retreat in the distance. At great speed I was pulled through the vastness of the Universe, and I developed an awareness of the majesty of God's creation. What I saw on my return trip to Earth would fill another book. I was amazed as I contemplated the wonders that I had been shown.

CHAPTER 13

▼

THE RETURN HOME

"Life is the first gift, love is the second,
and understanding is the third."

—*Marge Piercy*—

I felt myself snap back into my body, clearly aware of all that I had seen and experienced. Quickly I grabbed a pen and paper and began to record my memories in my journal. I feared that if this were a dream, then my experiences would just evaporate as the hours wore on. Exhausted by my efforts to record the experience, I fell into a deep sleep.

I awoke in my bed late the next morning with a reenergized feeling that my life would never be the same again. I rolled over and saw my open journal and felt a rush of memories flooding my mind. What had happened to me? Had I been to Heaven and back? Was it an actual trip or a dream? It really didn't matter.

Dreams can quickly evaporate, but the memory of that night has never diminished. I know without a doubt that I experienced an adventure in the afterlife that was as real as my life on Earth. In awe, I looked up to God and gave thanks for this journey of a lifetime that He gave me!

As I was lying in bed I thought about my experiences. I realized that we all have a mission in life beyond simply taking up space on planet Earth. Our mission is to be wise in our thoughts, words, and, certainly, in our deeds. Every person around each of us can be our teacher, and every one of us may in turn teach others.

We should seek wisdom from the great teachers and the many other wonderful people about us. Truth has the power to improve our lives and the lives of others who share our existence. God values wisdom from every mind and soul that conceives it, believes it, and achieves it.

I can say now that I have seen the Earth from afar, and it is not just a blue ball floating in space. Earth is our marvelous yet fragile planet. Each of us should feel privileged to be along for the journey. It is here on Earth that every one of us is tested daily, and given the free will to chart our own course.

Some would say that there is but one way to enter Heaven. Every one of us has been given a mind to ponder such things, and each can weigh the Truths. I believe that God has revealed through many teachers that each of us must find our personal way to Heaven. We choose our path to the great Truths. God said, "It's all about free will, choices, and the resulting quality of your spirit." And so it must be.

It was Shakespeare who said, "There are more things under Heaven and Earth than are dreamed of in our philosophies?" In this book I have shared that which I was inspired to write. What to do next is up to you. Believe as you choose, and remember that "The Last Passport to Heaven" is created by you. Your positive and negative actions will spread like ripples in a pond to many others around you. I hope that you find inspiration in this creation of paper and the wisdom presented in this book.

CHAPTER 14

THE GREAT WALL OF WISDOM ENGRAVED IN HEAVEN

Compilation & Title by Larry Richardson ©

Most of these messages were not used earlier. Please enjoy contemplating them at your leisure. Words are just the skins that surround a living idea and many great ideas are presented here. May this wisdom live in you.

God gave each of us the gift of life and what we do with our life is our gift to God.

—Anonymous—

"When one door closes, another door opens. But we often look so long at the closed door that we do not see the one, which just opened for us."

—Helen Keller—

"Triumph often is nearest when defeat seems inescapable."
—B.C. Forbes—

"Seek first to understand and then to be understood."
—St. Augustine—

It's unlucky to be superstitious.
—Gypsy Proverb—

"Small opportunities are often the start of great enterprises."
—Demosthenes—

"Never confuse a single defeat with a final defeat."
—F. Scott Fitzgerald—

"Lord, grant me the courage not to give up, even though I think it looks hopeless."
—Admiral Chester Nimitz—

"I was watching a sunset in Africa and I saw these words emblazoned on the sun, 'Have reverence for life.'"
—Albert Schweitzer—

"Faith without works is dead"
—BIBLE, James 2:36—

"You only learn when you are ready to listen."
—Anonymous—

"The price of wisdom is above rubies."
—BIBLE, Job 28:18—

"A friend is a gift that you give yourself."
—Robert Louis Stevenson—

"He that endureth to the end shall be saved."
—BIBLE, Matthew 10:22—

"Often the more you give away the more you have. It works with love, friendship, caring and sharing."
—Anonymous—

The smartest thing that I have ever said is help me! Help me!
—Anonymous—

Where your treasure is, there will your heart be also
—BIBLE, Matthew 6:21—

I have never been so rich that I could afford to lose a friend.
—Anonymous—

Get wisdom: and with all thy getting get understanding.
—BIBLE, Proverbs 4:7

You will either find a way or make a way
—Anonymous—

"The truth shall make you free"
BIBLE, John 8:32

"Anything that is of value in life only multiplies when it is given."
—Deepak Chopra—

"The love of truth has its reward in Heaven and even on Earth."
—Nietzche—

Visit often the homes of your friends, for the weeds will soon choke off the unused path.
—William Shakespeare—

Nine-tenths of wisdom is being wise in time
—Theodore Roosevelt—

"Truth's open to everyone, and the claims aren't all staked out yet."
—Seneca—

"If you seize every hour you seize the day."
—Sophocles—

"God's gift of the present is meant to be enjoyed right now."
—Larry Richardson—

"The past is the best prophet of the future."
—Lord Byron—

Gold is rare and valuable and not to be wasted. What about your precious time? How valuable is that?
—Larry Richardson—

The sky is not less blue because the blind man cannot see it.
—Danish Proverb—

"As he thinketh in his heart so is he."
—BIBLE, Proverbs 23:7

**"Live as though you were going to die tomorrow and learn as if
you will live forever."**
—Anonymous—

"Enthusiasm is faith in action"
— Anonymous—

"Then is then, and now is now. Learn the difference."
—Anonymous—

When glory comes memory departs.
—French Proverb—

One must lose one's life to find it.
—Anne Morrow Lindberg—

"If God should gift us with another day of life, let us make Him proud of how we used this gift."
—Larry Richardson—

"Sum up at night what you have done today."
—Lord Herbert—

"I dare you to knock the 'T' off can't."
—George Reeves—

"A clear conscience makes the softest pillow at night."
—Anonymous—

"Judge each day by the seeds that you plant, for God will judge you by what you produce."
—Larry Richardson—

"It is more blessed to give than receive"
—BIBLE, Acts 20:35

"People who can't be carried away, should be."
—Malcom Forbes—

"Do not curse the night, for without the night you couldn't see the stars."
—Anonymous—

"The oldest person alive is the person who has outlived his enthusiasm."
—H. David Thoreau—

"He did it with all his heart and prospered."
—BIBLE, 2 Chronicles 31:21—

"Wake up with a smile and go after life: Live it, enjoy it, taste it, smell it, feel it."
—Joe Knapp—

"A leader is a dealer of hope."
—Napoleon—

"Hope should be the last thing that you ever lose."
—Italian Proverb—

"Be a how thinker, not an if thinker."
—Anonymous—

Wise men learn by the mistakes of others. Fools learn by their own mistakes.
—H.G. Bohn—

When you are through changing, you're through.
—Bruce Barton—

The purpose of life is a life with purpose.
—Robert Byrne—

"Fear is a prison we build within ourselves to hold our
heart and mind captive."
—Larry Richardson—

"Courage is fear holding on one minute longer."
— George Patton—

Almost everything comes from almost nothing
—Henri Frederic Amiae—

He that is of a merry heart hath a continual feast.
—BIBLE, Proverbs 15:15—

"Courage is the golden key that unlocks the hold that fear
may have upon on us."
—Larry Richardson—

"Faith is God's work within us.
—St. Thomas Aquinas—

"When nothing is for sure, everything is possible."
—Margaret Drable—

If you can't accept losing you can't ever win.
—Vince Lombardi—

"Education is what remains after you have forgotten everything you learned."
—B.F. Skinner—

Many things are lost because nobody will ask.
—English Proverb—

The only people you should get even with are the people that helped you.
—Anonymous—

Kneeling will keep you in good standing.
—Anonymous—

"Fear knocked at the door and behold, no one was there."
—Anonymous—

The most precious words you can ever speak are words that uplift those less fortunate.
—Anonymous—

"How is it possible for you to be better dressed than when you wear a smile?"
—Larry Richardson—

"Prayer is less about changing the world around us than it is about changing ourselves."
—David Wolpe—

"Truth, like gold, is not less so for being newly brought out of the mine."
—John Locke—

"It is good to have an open mind, but not so open that when you bend over your brain falls out."
—Anonymous—

"When you teach children your wisdom you teach their children and their children also."
—Larry Richardson –

"Spring is God's way of saying. One more time!"
—Robert Orben—

"When the sun shines through your tears it often puts a rainbow on your heart."
—Anonymous—

"None are so empty as those who are full of themselves."
—Anonymous—

"Goodness is the only investment that never fails."
—Henry David Thoreau—

"I have never been so rich that I could afford to lose a friend."
—Anonymous—

"To teach is to learn twice over."
—Joseph Joubert—

"Speech is a mirror of the soul: as a man speaks so is he."
—Publilius Syrus—

"The best mirror is an old friend."
— Anonymous —

"It takes a long time to grow an old friend."
—John Leonard—

"A wish is desire without an attempt."
—Farmers Digest—

"Imagination is the true magic carpet."
—Norman Vincent Peale—

"For a great memory tomorrow make something special happen today."
—Larry Richardson—

"He who is bound to a star never turns back."
—Leonardo de Vinci—

"If you want to test the strength of your soul, try lifting someone who is down."
—Larry Richardson—

"How strange it is to use 'You only live once' as an excuse
to throw it all away."

—Bill Copeland—

"If you find a path with no obstacles it probably doesn't
lead
anyplace interesting."

—Frank Clark—

"It ain't over till it's over."

—Yogi Bera—

"Knowledge is power but enthusiasm pulls the switch."

—Ivern Ball—

Compliments cost little to give away. So why would a person hoard them like a miser?

—Larry Richardson –

"Apologies have great power to heal hurt, unless, of course, pride cuts in."
—Larry Richardson—

"You can't sweep others off their feet, if you can't be sweep off yours."
—Clarence Day—

"Having wisdom is having the ability to see miracles in the common."
—Ralph Waldo Emerson—

"Lord why haven't you sent someone to the Earth recently to make this a better place? The Lord replied, "I did, I sent you."
—Anonymous—

"Always try to do right. This will gratify some people, and astonish the rest."
—Mark Twain—

A soft answer turns away wrath.
—BIBLE, Proverbs 15:1—

"Be careful to make your words sweet because you may have to eat them someday."
—Anonymous—

"Don't let worry give a small thing a big shadow."
—Swedish Proverb—

"You only learn when you are willing to listen."
—Anonymous—

Resist the devil and he will flee from you.
—BIBLE, James 4:7—

"The greatest good that you can do for another person is not just share your riches but reveal to him or her their own."
—Benjamin Desraili—

"You'll never look big if you belittle."
—Dr. Gregory Richardson—

"Empathy is your pain in my heart."
—Jess Lair—

"Whatever your lot in life, build something on it."
—Home Life—

"Most worries are reruns."
—Claude McDonald—

"Encouragement doesn't make things happen, it happens to make things possible."
—Larry Richardson—

"Faith is building on what you know is here so you can reach what you know is there."
—Alden Hightower—

"If you want peace of mind, resign as General Manager of the Universe."
—Larry Eisenburg—

"Lord grant that I may always desire more than I can accomplish."
—Michelangelo—

"The darkest hour only has 60 minutes"
—Morris Mandell—

"True miracles are made by people who use the courage and intelligence that God gave them."
—Jean Anouilh—

"If you want to make a dream come true, then all you have to do is wake up."
—Anonymous—

"All the great things are simple and many are expressed in one word: Freedom, faith, justice, honor, duty, mercy, and hope."
—Winston Churchill—

"Make sure whatever you are doing in life is worth the precious time you are exchanging for it."
—Anonymous—

"The opportunities that God sends us do not wake up a sleeping person."
—Senegalese Proverb—

"Goals are dreams with deadlines."
—Diana Scharf Hunt—

"When I saw Heaven in her eyes, I just knew that she was an angelic soul."
—Larry Richardson—

"When it looks like your life is unraveling don't let the threads of faith and hope slip through your fingers."
—Larry Richardson—

"To know what is right to do and to do nothing is to lack courage."
—Anonymous—

"Ask and it will be given to you; seek and you shall find; knock and the door will open to you."
—Bible: Matthew 7:7—

"Every calling in life is great when greatly pursued."
—Oliver Wendell Holmes—

"Dying is easy, Comedy is hard."
—Edmund Gween—

"The two Chinese characters for crisis translate as 'dangerous and opportunity.'"
—John F. Kennedy—

There is nothing that cleanses the soul more than getting the hell kicked out of you."
—Woody Hayes—

"No one can say confidently that he will still be living tomorrow."
—Euripides—

"Judge each day by the seeds that you plant, for God will judge you by what you produce."
—Larry Richardson—

"What we think, we become."
—King Solomon—

"The greatest gift we can offer those in need is hope."
Daniel Beringer—

"A gem can't be polished without friction, or a person without trials."
—Anonymous—

"Small opportunities are often the start of great enterprises."
—Demosthenes—

"One loss is good for the soul. Too many loses are bad for the coach."

—Knute Rockne—

"Change your thoughts and you change the world."

—Norman Vincent Peale—

"Faith is the soul's adventure."

—William Bridges—

"The greatest gift that you can give another is your focused attention."

—Richard Moss M.D.—

"Success seems largely a matter of hanging on after others have let go."

—William Feather—

"Why not go out on a limb? Isn't that where the fruit is?"
—Anonymous—

"When nothing is for sure, everything is possible."
—Margaret Drable—

"Those who bring light into the lives of others cannot keep it from themselves."
—Helen Keller—

"Faith is God's work within us."
—Anonymous—

"Those who are truly happy have learned to serve others."
—Albert Schweitzer—

"So get a few laughs and do the best that you can."
—Will Rodgers—

"If life should teach you something positive, honor the wisdom and share it often with others."
—Anonymous—

"Every person must get to Heaven in their own way."
—Frederick The Great—

"If you haven't discovered something worth dying for then you haven't really lived."
—Martin Luther King, Jr.—

"Of course I am an optimist, I haven't learned enough to be pessimistic yet."
—Anonymous—

"Good intentions have often been used to pave the fast lane to Hell."
—Anonymous—

"All that I have seen teaches me to trust the creator for all that I have not seen."
—Ralph Waldo Emerson—

"Each one of us who travels further than the obstacles will know a different kind of life from that time on."
—J. Stone—

"Every problem contains the seed of its own solution."
—Stanley Arnold—

"God constantly speaks to us through each other, as well as from within."
—Thomas Keating—

"Almost everything comes from almost nothing."
—Henri Frederick Amiae—

"Only one man in 1,000 is a leader of men —The other 999 follow women."
—Groucho Marx—

"I can live two months on a good compliment."
—Mark Twain—

"As you think, so you are and as you choose, so you will be."
—Henry James—

"Would the boy or girl that you once were be proud of the man or woman you are today?"
—Anonymous—

"God gave each of us the gift of life and what we do with our life is our gift to God."
—Anonymous—

"The best things in life are not things."
—Art Buchwald—

"There are two ways to spread the light; be a candle or the mirror that reflects it."
—Edith Wharton—

"Faith embraces many truths which seem at times to contradict each other."
—Blaine Pascal-

"Be careful how you live, you may be the only bible that some people ever read."
—Anonymous—

B.I.B.L.E.=Basic Instructions Before Leaving Earth.
—Anonymous—

"Whether you think you can or can't, you're right!"
—Henry Ford—

"Ignorant people don't know what good they hold in their hands until they have flung it away."
—Sophocles—

"Who is blinder than the person who will not see?"
—Andrew Boarde—

"Love, laughter, praise, and confidence are all contagious, but so are the opposites of each word. Make sure you share the best of you, not the worst."
—Larry Richardson—

"Goodness is the only investment that never fails."
—Henry David Thoreau—

See Appendix One to record your own wisdom in this book

Looking Up!

When searching your soul
For the truth about you

Celebrate the good
Seek improvements to do

Don't ever give up
To your own self be true

The Last Passport to Heaven
Is created by you

—Larry R. Richardson—

EPILOGUE

SHARING THE PASSPORT TO HEAVEN

"If you want to test the strength of your soul try lifting up someone who is down."

—Larry Richardson—

I have shared "The Last Passport to Heaven" for over 35 years. Others have delighted at the revelation of the "Passport" on numerous airplane flights, National Conventions, in homes, at churches, and on the streets.

I urge you to share "The Last Passport to Heaven" with others. It is an amazing paper creation that instills a childlike wonder. Smiles are generated as the paper unfolds. When presenting "The Last Passport to Heaven," feel free to create a story based on your own personal beliefs; a short version about going to Heaven can be shared in a brief period of time.

As you convey the wisdom of the message through your story telling skills utilize the power of your enthusiasm. Enthusiasm is an ancient concept over 3,000 years old. It comes from the Greek words "En Theos" which translates as having God or spirit within. Use "The Passport to Heaven" to help express the spirit within you to others.

This book has been a labor of love, which has been 35 years in the making. Many experiences from my own life have been incorporated into this story including several profound meditation experiences. I am particularly pleased with the wisdom I have gathered over a lifetime to share with you the reader.

I hope that you enjoyed this story and the remarkable "The Last Passport to Heaven." Although our own spiritual and life beliefs are very personal to each of us, we can celebrate the general themes, which celebrate our humanity and our faith.

Appendix

Appendix One

A Wisdom Journal

Compiled by: _____ Start Date: _____

Here is a section for you to record your favorite phrases, truths or insights of wisdom. Once you record it make sure you share it with others. If you don't use it, you can lose it.

_____

_____

_____

_____

_____

_____

_____

_____

_____

_____

_____

_____

_____
_____
_____
_____
_____
_____
_____
_____
_____
_____
_____
_____
_____
_____
_____
_____
_____
_____
_____
_____
_____
_____
_____
_____
_____

Congratulations! You certainly have an appreciation for wisdom. Don't forget to record those wise sayings from your own family and friends before they get lost. It might be wise to get a special book if you have filled these pages up. Be a collector, implementer and disseminator of wisdom.

Appendix

Appendix Two

"My Words of Life" Reader Note:

Following this page you will find "My Words for Life" list which Aaron explained early in his story. This listing represents words that are uplifting and energizing to Aaron the author of the Journal.

I recommend that if you would like to create a list like this, type on a computer or write down on paper each word that you enjoy. Keep writing these words until you have exhausted your present supply. As you come up with additional words you may add them at will.

I believe that you will find the "Words for Life" to be an inspiring exercise which can encourage your hopes, dreams, thoughts, and actions to come forth wisely. I have included two pages in this book for you to try this exercise.

Enjoy creating your own "Words for Life" list.

Sincerely,

Larry R. Richardson
Author "The Last Passport to Heaven"

APPENDIX

AARON'S "WORDS FOR LIFE" LIST

Acceptance
Acting
Action
Adventure
Alaska
Appreciation
Aromas
Autumn
Belief
Birds
Camping
Canoeing
Caring
Children
Chocolate
Clouds

Collectibles
Comedy
Conversation
Cookies
Cruising
Dessert
Dolphins
Dreaming
Driving
Enthusiasm
Esteem
Europe
Family
Faith
Fireplace
Flowers

Flying
Food
Football
Forest
Forgiveness
Friends
Friendship
Fun
Games
Gifts
Giving
Glaciers
Guitar
Heartfelt
Hiking
Historical

Hope	Pondering	Space
Lakes	Radiance	Speaking
Laughter	Rafting	Spirit
Learning	Rain	Spring
Love	Rainbows	Summer
Magic	Reading	Sunrise
Massage	Rest	Sunsets
Meditating	Sequoias	Sunshine
Money	Sharing	Swimming
Movies	Showers	Tahoe
Music	Singing	Television
Painting	Sky	Traveling
Parents	Sleeping	Vision
Passion	Smiles	Waterfalls
Peace	Snorkeling	Waves
Photography	Snow	Wind
Play	Soul	

APPENDIX

CREATE YOUR OWN WORDS FOR LIFE LIST

_____   _____   _____
_____   _____   _____
_____   _____   _____
_____   _____   _____
_____   _____   _____
_____   _____   _____
_____   _____   _____
_____   _____   _____
_____   _____   _____
_____   _____   _____
_____   _____   _____
_____   _____   _____

Appendix

Appendix Three

The Way of Three Crosses

Reader Instruction #10 and Illustration #8

To create the **"Way of the Three Crosses"** mentioned earlier in this book you will need an additional sheet of 8 ½ by 11 inch white paper and a pair of scissors. The following diagram visually shows you each step.

Step 1.   Create a new Passport as shown earlier in Illustration #1

Step 2.   Use a pencil and divide the Passport into 3 equal sections by drawing two light lines.

Step 3.   Cut along the lines from the top down until you are about one inch from the bottom of the folded paper.

Step 4.   Cut across the bottom of the two lines and remove the paper pieces. These pieces will be used in step 6.

Step 5.   Open up the paper you see in step 4 and reveal the large cross in the center and two poles along the side.

Step 6.   Open all the pieces of paper you have left and complete the crosses on the left and right of the large center cross. Overlay any extra pieces of paper until all your pieces are gone.

This paper creation is a symbolic reminder of the sacrifice that Jesus made at Calvary for mankind and the forgiveness of sins for those who believe.

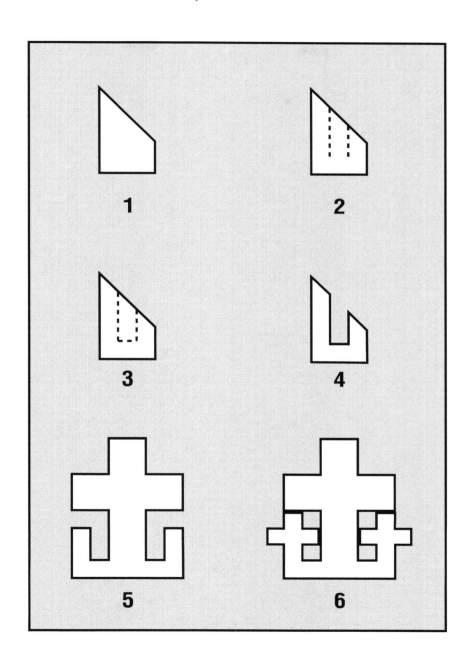

INDEX

Alphabetical Index of Authors Quoted
Where the Source Was Known

Forbes, Malcom, 72
Ford, Henry, 95
Frederick The Great, 91
Gween, Edmund, 87
Hayes, Woody, 87
Hemmingway, Ernest, 34
Herbert, Lord, 71
Hightower, Alden, 84
Holmes, Oliver Wendell, 87
Home Life, 62, 83
Hunt, Diana Scharf, 86
James, Henry, 52, 93
Joubert, Joseph, 78
Keating, Thomas, 92
Keller, Helen, 65, 90
Kennedy, John F., 87
King, Martin Luther Jr., 91
Knapp, Joe, 72
Lair, Jess, 83
Leonard, John, 78
Lessing, G.E.*****
Lindberg, Anne Morrow, 71
Locke, John, 76
Lombardi, Vince, 75
Mandell, Morris, 84
Marx, Groucho, 93
McDonald, Claude, 83
Moss, Richard M.D.*****
Napoleon, 73
Nietzche, 68
Nimitz, Admiral Chester, 66
Orben, Robert, 77

Pascal, Blaine*****
Patton, George, 74
Peale, Norman Vincent, 79, 89
Piercy, Marge, 62
Postman, Neil, vii
Reeves, George, 71
Richardson, Gregory M.D.*****
Richardson, Larry, 3, 7, 9, 11, 13, 19, 21, 23, 25, 29, 31, 33, 35, 39, 41, 43, 45, 47, 49, 51, 53, 55, 57, 59, 61, 63-65, 67, 69, 71, 73-77, 79-81, 83-89, 91, 93, 95, 97, 101, 111, 115
Rockne, Knute, 89
Rogers, Will*****
Roosevelt, Theodore, 68
Schweitzer, Albert, 66, 90
Seneca, 69
Shakespeare, William, 68
Skinner, B.F., 75
Solomon King*****
Sophocles, 69, 95
St. Augustine, 65
St. Thomas Aquinas, 74
Stevenson, Robert Louis, 12, 66
Stone, J., 92
Syrus, Publilius, 78
Thoreau, Henry David, 78, 95
Twain, Mark, 9, 29, 81, 93
Well, Albert M. Jr.*****
Wharton, Edith, 94
Wolpe, David, 76

ABOUT THE AUTHOR

Larry Richardson was born in 1948 in Cadillac, Michigan and was raised in his hometown of Midland, Michigan. He received his degree in Business Administration from Central Michigan University in 1970. Larry has served for over 27 years as CEO of a number of non-profit, human service organizations in Michigan, Florida, California and Hawaii. "The Last Passport to Heaven" was the result of a story first told to the author by his mother Dora in the 1960's. This book also incorporates meditation experiences, which the author had in the 1970's while living in Hawaii.

The author's interests include: Meditation, spiritual development, public speaking, filmmaking, travel, and service to others. Over a period of 35 years Larry has shared "The Passport to Heaven" with hundreds of youth and adults throughout the world. Larry is single and has one daughter Brie.

You can reach the author at this e-mail address:
thelastpassporttoheaven@yahoo.com

Made in the USA
San Bernardino, CA
14 April 2016